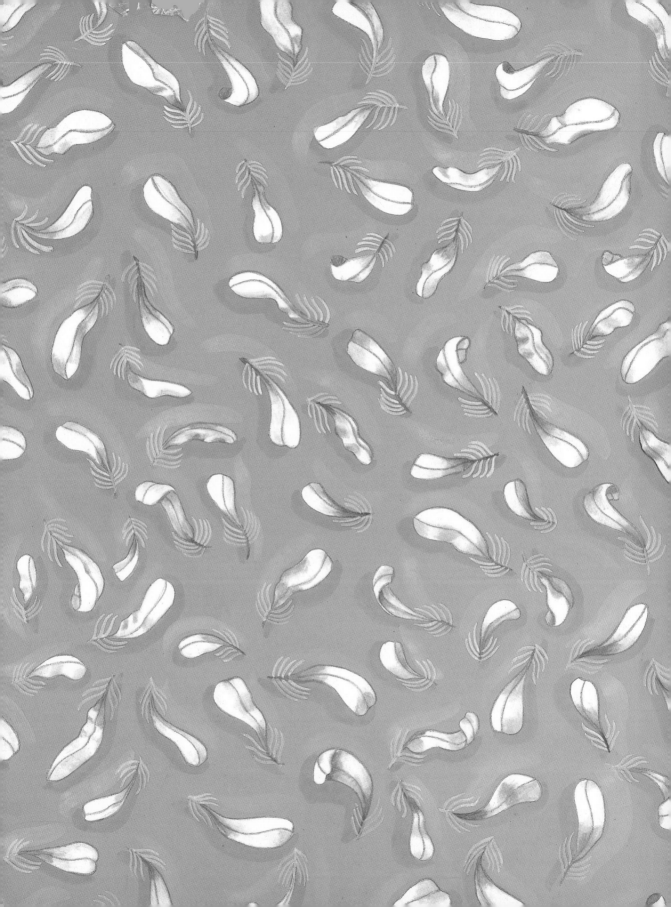

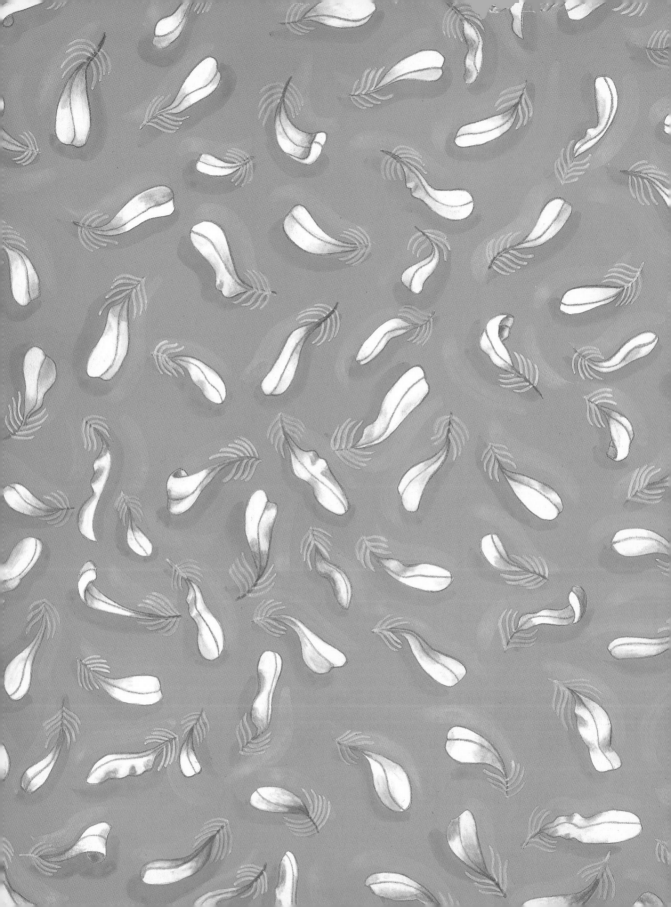

JOAN ROTHENBERG

Yettele's Feathers

Hyperion Books for Children
New York

FIRST EDITION

1 3 5 7 9 10 8 6 4 2

Library of Congress Cataloging-in-Publication Data

Rothenberg, Joan — Yettele's feathers / retold and illustrated by Joan Rothenberg — 1st ed.   p.   cm.
Summary: Yettele, who loves to gossip, is finally taught a lesson by the Rabbi. ISBN
0-7868-0097-6 (trade) — ISBN 0-7868-2081-0 (lib. bdg.)   [1. Jews — Folklore.   2. Folklore —
Europe, Eastern.]   I. Title.   PZ8.1.R74Ye   1995   398.2′089924   dc20 — [E]   94–26623

The artwork for each picture is prepared using gouache on bristol board.
This book is set in 18-point Stempel Schneidler.
Book design by Joann Hill Lovinski.

For my beloved teachers, Barbara and Miriam,
and most especially Arleen

As towns go, Ostrow was rather on the small side. In fact, it was said that if you were riding in a wagon and happened to sneeze just as you were entering Ostrow, you'd be out of town again before you could open your eyes and wipe your nose. So when Yettele Babbelonski looked out her window, she could see the whole town.

Yettele lived in a tiny room over the baker's shop. She had no children, and her husband, Mendel, "may he rest in peace!" had died. With no one to care for but herself, Yettele had a lot of time for minding other people's business.

More than anything else, Yettele loved to talk. She loved the sound and feel of the words as they rolled off her tongue. It didn't much matter that she had no one at home to listen. She talked to herself, to the walls and the furniture, and even to the carrots and sweet potatoes as she was cutting them into the *tzimmes.*

"Cut and chop, cut and chop. Quick, crispy carrots hop into the pot!"

When she grew tired of talking to walls and chairs, she put on her babushka and shawl and went outside. She talked to anyone who would listen.

Now, everyone likes to hear a good story, especially when it happens to be about someone they know. But, as time went by, people started hearing stories about themselves and they didn't like it one bit.

"My poor Goldie," cried Moe Pishkin. "Nobody will eat her delicious chicken soup — ever since Yettele started spreading those rumors that she adds sawdust to make her matzo balls bigger!"

"*Gottenyu!*" cried Tillie Schnitzele, the dressmaker. "How can I make a living with Yettele telling all of the ladies that I fit their dresses too small on purpose, just to make them feel fat?"

There were many others who felt the sting of
Yettele's gossip, but the story she told about Yussel
Farfel was the last straw! One Friday morning she
watched from her window as people bought their
chickens and challahs and candles for Shabbat. She
saw Yussel take an apple as he passed the fruit stand.

"*Nu?*" remarked Yettele to the chair. "What is
Yussel Farfel doing wandering around town taking
apples?

"Poor Fanny Farfel," sighed Yettele. "Five children
to care for and a husband who is forced to steal apples
to feed his family."

By the time this story got around, one apple had become a whole bagful and poor Yussel was very nearly fired from his job in the butcher's shop! His reputation was sorely bruised.

"Yettele Babbelonski, you thoughtless old busybody!" cried Fanny, her face red as a beet. "May all of your teeth fall out except for one — and in that one you should have a toothache! Maybe then your mouth will be too busy for such preposterous lies!

"First of all, my Yussel took only *one* apple, not a whole bagful. And he didn't steal it, either. Yussel delivered a fat chicken to Sophie, the grocer's wife. Tevye offered Yussel the apple in exchange for the favor."

"Fanny Farfel, there's no need to get so upset," said Yettele. "I didn't mean to cause any trouble. I didn't see Yussel deliver the chicken to Sophie. I'm very sorry and I take it all back!"

"The damage has already been done," snapped Fanny. "You can't just take it back! Don't you have anything better to do than sit in that window of yours and poke your nose into other people's business?"

Soon there wasn't a soul in Ostrow who felt safe from Yettele's wagging tongue.

"There's old Blabbermouth Babbelonski!" people cried when they saw her. They would stop talking and walk in the opposite direction.

One day Yettele had a particularly spicy tidbit about Moishe Mushnik and his shoe. She was just itching to tell it to someone. Finding no one who cared to listen, she decided to visit the Rabbi.

"The Rabbi is never too busy to listen," she told herself, "and he never turns anyone away."

"Yettele Babbelonski, it's so nice to see you," greeted the Rabbi. "What brings you here to see me today?"

"I have this remarkable tale to tell about Moishe Mushnik's shoe, but nobody will listen," said Yettele. "No one will even talk to me and I don't know why. Rabbi, please, I need your help!"

The Rabbi knew exactly why no one would talk to Yettele. "Those tall tales of hers," he thought to himself and pulled on his beard. "But—what to do? What to do!"

"My dear Yettele," he began. "It occurs to me that some people might be hurt by your stories."

"Hurt by my stories?" cried Yettele. "*My goodness!* They're only words, not rocks and stones. What harm can come from a word? Certainly no more harm than from a feather!"

"I think that I can help," said the Rabbi. "But first, I must ask you to help me with a problem."

"It would be an honor," replied Yettele. "Just ask and it is done!"

"Please, go home and find the biggest and plumpest pillow you have. Take some scissors and cut off the top," instructed the Rabbi. "When you've done that, bring the pillow to me."

"Such an odd request," muttered Yettele to herself as she hurried home. "But he is the Rabbi, a very wise man. Who am I to question?"

Even so, she did feel rather foolish cutting the top off a perfectly good pillow.

Yettele took the pillow and set out for the Rabbi's house. Just as she stepped out into the street, a particularly rambunctious gust of wind came up from behind and snatched the pillow right out of her arms. Before she knew what hit her, Yettele was lost in a blizzard of goose feathers!

Yettele ran after the pillow but by the time she caught it, it was almost empty. She grabbed handfuls of feathers that had drifted into the gutters and tried to stuff them back into the pillow.

"*Oy vey!* What am I going to do now?" she wailed. "I'd better take what's left of this pillow to the Rabbi before it gets any smaller."

The Rabbi tried to hide his amusement as he opened his door to find Yettele, with goose feathers stuck to her clothing and tangled in her hair. In her hands she carried the limp remains of her finest pillow.

"Yettele, you disappoint me," he scolded. "Is this the biggest pillow you could find?"

"But Rabbi, this is my very best pillow. You couldn't find a finer pillow in all of Ostrow!" protested Yettele. "You told me to cut the top off, so I cut the top off. Is it my fault that the wind came and blew away all the feathers? Rabbi, I've done what you asked. Now, won't you please help me?"

"I can't help you until you go out and find all of the feathers and put them back into the pillow," explained the Rabbi.

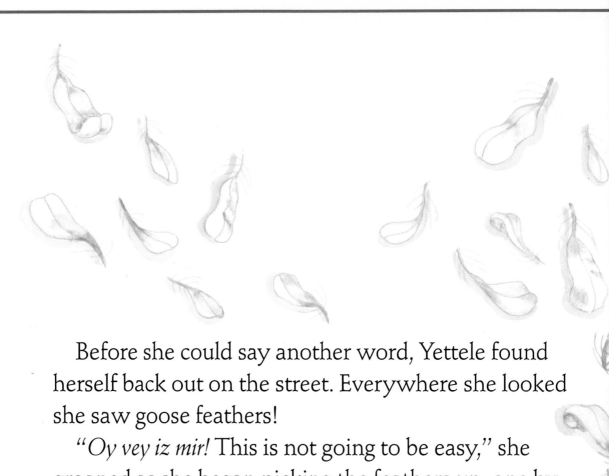

Before she could say another word, Yettele found herself back out on the street. Everywhere she looked she saw goose feathers!

"*Oy vey iz mir!* This is not going to be easy," she groaned as she began picking the feathers up, one by one, and stuffing them back into the pillow.

Yettele spent the rest of the day picking feathers up off the street and out of the gutters, off the heels of people's boots and out of the tails of all the horses. She picked feathers out of the hay and the billy goats' beards. She shook feathers out of the trees and swept them off the windowsills.

By the time the sun was setting, Yettele's back and fingers and eyes were aching. She was dead on her feet, and still the pillow was only half full.

She dragged her aching bones back to the Rabbi's house. She was cold and tired and hungry, and she didn't feel like talking at all!

"Yettele, it's so late, I was sure you had gone home long ago," said the Rabbi. "Please come in and rest yourself." He invited her to sit down and offered her some tea and *ruggelach*. Yettele sipped her tea gratefully and gobbled down three of the delicious sweet pastries.

"Rabbi, I've been picking up feathers for hours and hours," sighed Yettele. "If I spend the rest of my days picking up feathers, I could never put them all back into the pillow."

A smile spread across the Rabbi's face. "And so it is with those stories of yours, my dear Yettele. Once the words leave your lips, they are as impossible to put back as those feathers!"

Ostrow was never completely rid of Yettele's feathers. People were picking them out of their shops and houses for weeks, though it wasn't long before they went unnoticed.

Yettele began to tell new stories. They were stories about herself. They were about when she was a girl, before she married Mendel "may he rest in peace!" and moved to Ostrow.

Everyone loved these stories, but Yettele's greatest fans were the children. Every day they flocked up to Yettele's cozy little room, where she spent hours filling them with freshly baked strudel and marvelous tales.

Of course, the story that everyone loved the best was the one about the feathers. Each time Yettele told it, she was reminded to think about her words before they left her lips forever!

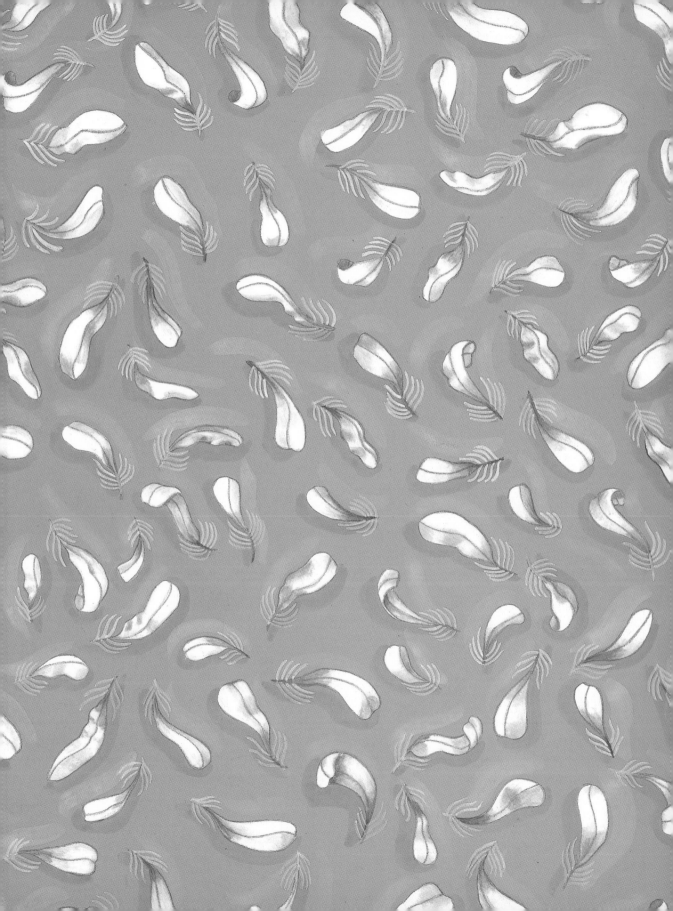

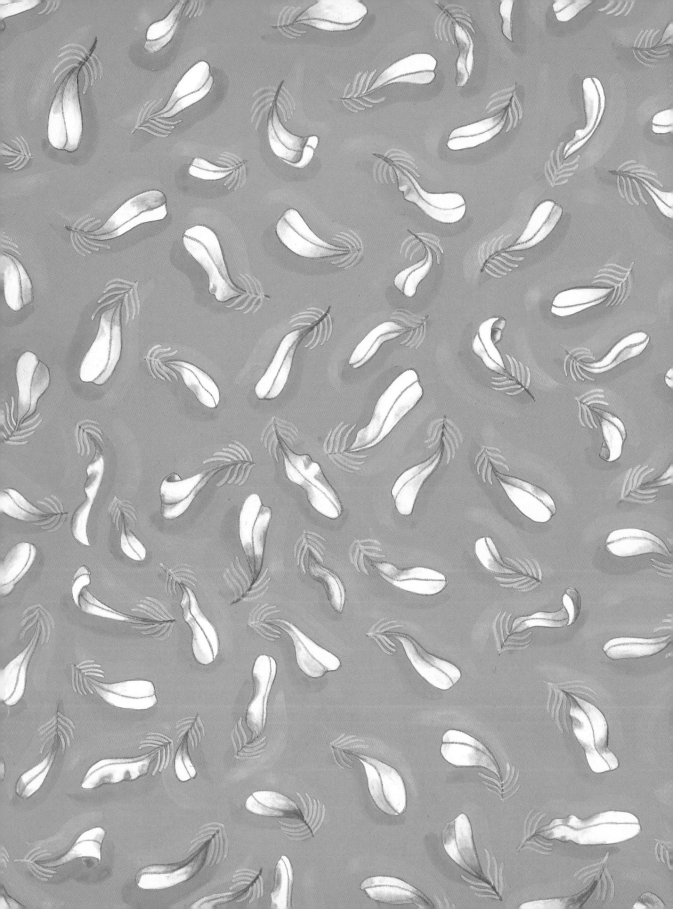